A King Production presents…

ASSASSINS HOLIDAY…

EPISODE 4
(Silent Night, Savage Winter)

JOY DEJA KING

ISBN 10: 1-958834-42-4
ISBN 13: 978-1-958834-42-80
Graphic design: www.anitaart79.wixsite.com/bookdesign
Typesetting: Anita J.

Cover concept by Joy Deja King
Cover model: Joy Deja King
Library of Congress Cataloging-in-Publication Data;
A King Production
Assassins Silent Night, Savage Winter...Bad Bitches Only by Joy Deja King
For complete Library of Congress Copyright info visit;
www.joydejaking.com
Twitter @joydejaking

A King Production
P.O. Box 912, Collierville, TN 38027
A King Production and the above portrayal log are trademarks of A King Production LLC

This Book is Dedicated To My:

Family, Readers and Supporters.
I LOVE you guys so much. Please believe that!!

--Joy Deja King

"This Christmas, Survival Is
The Only Tradition…"

ASSASSINS HOLIDAY...

EPISODE 4
(Silent Night, Savage Winter)

JOY DEJA KING

Chapter One

THE GIRL WHO WASN'T SUPPOSED TO LIVE

Atlanta rarely saw snow, but tonight the sky flirted with it, thin gray clouds drifting low, heavy like they were threatening to burst open. Hartsfield-Jackson swarmed with holiday chaos, families decked in coordinated sleepwear, executives shouting quarterly projections into cell phones, visitors documenting their travels against the towering, glittering pine. Not one of them noticed her, the shadow moving through automatic doors, face obscured beneath a deep hood, infant secured against her body like the most precious contraband.

Invisible by design. Dead women don't travel with babies. Shiffon glided through the terminal, pace deliberate, quick enough to blend with holiday travelers, measured enough to avoid attention. Her pulse drowned out the airport symphony of roller bags and gate changes. Against her chest, her son's tiny body rose and fell with each breath, her chest, his warmth seeped through layers of fabric, his breath a gentle rhythm against her skin. One tiny fist had worked free of his swaddle, five perfect fingers unfurled in sleep, their shape and length unmistakable. A genetic echo. Maverick's hands, reborn.

Maverick haunted her from the grave, his ghost living in every feature of her son's face, the curve of his nose, the set of that tiny jawline, those eyes that opened like dark knives, cutting through the world with unnatural awareness. Her boots struck the curb as December's chill bit at her skin, hostile and unforgiving. Atlanta had transformed while she was gone. Harsher now. Stripped bare. The city wore its holiday decorations like costume jewelry, twinkling lights, evergreen wreaths on every lamppost, windows frosted with artificial snow, but beneath the seasonal disguise, she felt the truth: this place remained what it had always been, a foundation of concrete stained with memories of blood.

Eyes darting beneath the veil of her hood, Shiffon scanned the pick-up lane with practiced precision. Family piling into a minivan. Driver holding an

Uber sign. Lovers tangled against each other by the crosswalk, oblivious to the world. No vehicles idling too long. No eyes lingering where they shouldn't. No midnight-black Charger purring at the curb. No ghosts from the life she'd fled.

The burner in her pocket vibrated once, not a call or text, but the silent alert she dreaded from one of her paid informants confirming someone was hunting for border-crossing women with newborns. Ice flooded her veins.

It could only be Riot, Maverick's attack dog, now masterless and rabid with grief. His unhinged protege, too young, too volatile, desperate to prove himself worthy of the crown he'd inherited. Dangerous because he had nothing to lose and everything to prove. The kind of man who'd burn cities searching for a ghost. The kind who'd kill to possess what remained of his mentor's bloodline.

Shiffon pressed her lips to the baby's forehead. "We safe now, little man. Almost there."

The rideshare's headlights swept across her as it pulled to the curb. A Toyota with peeling stickers. Behind the wheel sat an older Black man, eyes heavy with late-shift fatigue, a crooked Santa hat perched on his gray-flecked hair. He popped the trunk with a mechanical thunk, then watched through the rearview as she secured the carrier in the backseat.

"Coming home for the holidays?" his voice carried the practiced warmth of someone who'd asked the same question fifty times today.

Home. The word pierced her. Her throat tightened.

She saw her mother's kitchen, the way it smelled like cinnamon this time of year. Pictured her brother, sixteen now, probably with a new growth spurt, walking these streets believing his sister was ash and memory. Both living three miles from where she sat, keeping a dead girl's Christmas stocking in the attic. The shrine they must have made of her things, photos, her favorite earrings, maybe that graduation tassel she'd hung from the mirror.

The car merged into traffic. Through the window, the airport terminals receded, replaced by Atlanta's skyline, holiday lights winking like false stars.

"Just visiting," she said softly.

Her chest ached with the thought of her mother cradling her baby, those familiar hands that had once braided her hair now touching her son's cheeks, singing those same lullabies. But a grandmother's joy would become a death sentence. Her son wasn't just a miracle, a gift, he was evidence. Evidence she'd survived. Evidence Maverick's blood still flowed through veins. Evidence men would kill to possess. Evidence Maverick's legacy was breathing, and it was worth killing for.

"Where to?" the driver adjusted his hat.

She passed a creased paper forward. "This address. Take the back roads, though. Highways jammed this time of night."

And lined with traffic cams, facial recognition, she thought.

The driver nodded, Santa hat bobbing. "Your ride, your route."

She leaned over the carrier, adjusting the blanket's edge. Her son's eyelids fluttering as if chasing warmth and safety that existed nowhere but inside of him. His mouth making tiny movements like he was tasting something sweet in his dreams, oblivious to the harsh reality surrounding his bubble of innocence.

"Half the city would kill to claim you," she whispered against his ear, words dissolving into breath. "And you just got here."

Her phone vibrated again. Another update from her informant. Whisper from the streets. More noise about Maverick's "seed." Word was spreading through Atlanta's underground about his legacy. Questions circled like vultures. Had the man who terrorized the streets left behind more than bullet holes and fear? Had his woman gotten pregnant before the chaos? Had she escaped with his child, or had death claimed them both? The truth slept inches away, oblivious to his own power.

The car sliced through neighborhoods where Christmas bled across windows in crimson and emerald streaks, now melting under tentative snowfall. Atlanta rarely dressed in white; these weren't blizzard flakes but hesitant messengers, as if winter itself approached with caution. "Silent Night" drifted from the radio as the driver's fingers tapped the steering wheel. Children wrestled fresh-cut pines toward front doors. A plastic holy family glowed electric blue, their savior dusted with artificial powder.

Shiffon's fingernail carved a crescent into her palm, anchoring her to the moment. Calculate. Execute. Survive. Reach sanctuary. Essence with her tactical mind. Bailey's unflinching loyalty. Leila's network of shadows. The only three women who'd risk everything to shelter Maverick McClay's son and the ghost who bore him. The only ones who'd defy Genesis Taylor himself, the man who ordered her death. His voice still frosted her spine and echoed in her nightmares. Those four words, cold, unbothered, delivered without emotion: "Take care of it."

Genesis was in a hospital now, clinging to life. The thought should have comforted her, but it didn't. His body might be tethered to machines, but his influence still pulsed through the city's veins. A man like that didn't need consciousness to execute plans already in motion. He had contingency plans for his own death. His empire would keep hunting even while he slept.

"Coming up on it now," the driver announced, steering onto a quiet tree-lined street. "This the spot?"

"That's it." The building matched Leila's photos exactly, brick facade with weathered charm, security door with chipped paint, Christmas lights strung haphazardly across some balconies, a mix of economy sedans and work trucks parked curbside. Nothing flashy.

Nothing that screamed target. The car eased to the curb, and her heartbeat quickened in response.

She handed him folded bills. "Appreciate it."

His eyes met hers in the rearview. "Stay safe out there," he said, adjusting his Santa hat. "Holidays bring out all kinds of crazy."

Don't I know it. "We will," she promised.

Shiffon stepped out into the cold, flurries melting on her cheeks. The December air bit at her face, snowflakes dissolving against her skin like tiny surrenders. Before her stood the building, solid, anonymous, unremarkable except for the crooked wreath on 2B and the muffled sound of a sitcom's canned laughter filtering through someone's window. Shiffon readjusted her son's carrier against her chest, inhaling deeply as if oxygen might somehow fortify her against what waited inside." Here we go, baby boy," she murmured against his forehead. "Time to meet the cavalry."

Every cell in her body vibrated with uncertainty: she'd already played dead once. The universe wouldn't grant her another resurrection.

Chapter Two

DON'T OPEN THAT DOOR

Shiffon stood in front of the nondescript building, her heart pounding in her ears, the weight of her son against her chest grounding her in the reality of the danger that surrounded them. She took a deep breath, the icy air burning her lungs, the taste of snowflakes on her lips a bitter reminder of the precariousness of their situation.

With a sense of purpose, she pushed open the entrance door and stepped into the dimly lit hallway. The muffled sounds of life behind closed doors drifted to her ears, a stark contrast to the silence that enveloped her own fears. Her mind raced with thoughts of the past she had left behind the present dangers that lurked in the shadows, and the uncertain future that lay ahead.

As she made her way down the corridor, each step echoing in the quiet, she finally reached apartment 2B, Shiffon paused, her heart hammering in her chest. This was it. She was about to reunite with Essence, Leila, and Bailey, the women who had mourned her.

Bailey was halfway through a glass of merlot and watching some mindless reality show when the knock came. Her finger found the mute button as she frowned toward the door. In the kitchen, Essence's stream of commentary about some pseudo-intellectual Instagram personality cut off mid-laugh. Leila's head appeared from the bedroom doorway, satin scarf wrapped tight, one eyebrow climbing her forehead.

"You got company coming?" Bailey asked the room.

"Hell no," Essence replied, voice tight with suspicion.

"And who's out here knocking like they contribute to the rent?"

The second knock landed differently, three deliberate taps. Unhurried. Controlled. Almost composed.

"Probably just your takeout habit showing up," Bailey said, rising and setting her wine aside with a pointed look at Essence.

"First, stay out my business," Essence shot back,

hand pressed dramatically to her chest. "And second, I'm on a spending freeze this week. Ain't ordered nothing."

Leila emerged fully, adjusting the waistband of her sweatpants. "Maybe it's that delivery I mentioned?" she suggested, though uncertainty colored her voice.

A single look passed between them in three heartbeats, bodies tensing in practiced unison. Essence's hand drifted toward the kitchen drawer—the one with Chinese menus on top, cold steel underneath. Leila palmed her phone, thumb poised over contacts that could summon men who answered at 3 AM with questions second, violence first. Bailey approached the door, each step calculated to avoid the creaky floorboard. Another knock.

"Just a minute," Bailey called, voice honeyed yet wary.

The response came muffled through wood. Soft. Exhausted. Hauntingly recognizable. "It's me."

Bailey's breath caught. Impossible.

"Who?" Essence mouthed across the room.

Bailey's fingers trembled against the peephole. She looked, then stumbled backward.

"Bailey?" Leila's whisper cut through the silence. "Tell us."

"It's Shiffon," Bailey said, the words barely escaping her throat. The name itself a resurrection. "She's alive."

The apartment suspended in disbelief. Essence's

wineglass wobbled dangerously against marble before finding balance. Leila's face transformed with a vulnerability Bailey had never witnessed, raw, unguarded shock.

"You better not be playing. "Don't joke about shit like that," Essence started advancing.

"I swear," Bailey said, voice cracking. "And she's not alone. She's holding..." The words stuck. "She's holding a baby."

"A baby?" Leila repeated, the question hanging between them like smoke. Nobody breathed.

Leila's voice cracked. "A baby? Like an actual infant?"

For a moment the room froze in a tableau of disbelief. Essence then nudged Bailey aside with her hip and pressed her eye to the peephole. Her hand flew to her mouth. There stood Shiffon, hood shadowing her face, dark circles beneath eyes that had seen too much. Her cheeks had lost their fullness. Against her chest, a bundle in a carrier, five tiny fingers visible, curling and uncurling against the edge of a blanket. Essence's back found the wall, her palm flat against it for support.

"Unfuckin' believable," she breathed. "It's her."

Another knock, gentler than before. Uncertain.

"Get her inside," Leila commanded through clenched teeth. "Someone could walk by any second."

Bailey snapped from her trance. She turned the deadbolt, opened the door scanning the hallway. Clear. No lurking figures, no footsteps, no watching eyes.

Only Shiffon in her threadbare jacket, melting snow caught in her eyelashes. Bailey grabbed her wrist and pulled her through the doorway, securing the lock behind them with the fluid motion of someone who'd checked windows and doors her entire life.

Shiffon stumbled forward, the apartment's warmth enveloping her, incense, coconut oil, and yesterday's takeout containers creating a familiar perfume she no longer had rights to. The silence stretched between them, taut as wire.

Essence lunged forward first, gripping Shiffon's shoulders with trembling fingers, her eyes glassy, swimming between rage and relief.

"Bitch," she whispered. "You better tell me this ain't no ghost."

Shiffon let out a tired, broken laugh. "If I'm a ghost, hell ghetto as fuck," she rasped. "Y'all got the heat on a hundred. Somebody turn down the thermostat in the afterlife," she managed with her dry humor. "Burning up in here."

Essence's composure cracked. She pulled Shiffon into her arms, mindful of the baby between them.

"The nerve," she murmured, voice muffled against Shiffon's collar. "Playing dead and then walking back in here like the second coming."

Leila appeared at their side, fingers fluttering near the baby, her voice soft. "The little one...is he okay?"

Shiffon tilted just enough to reveal her son's face.

His dark eyes tracked the unfamiliar faces surrounding him, tiny features pinching with what looked like masculine suspicion.

"Yeah, he surviving," Shiffon whispered, her voice a mixture of fierce protection and exhaustion. "Been through storms already, but he's holding on."

Bailey's throat tightened as she approached. "Would you mind if..." Her hands made a cradling motion.

With a nod, Shiffon peeled back the blanket's edge.

"My son," she said softly. "Still working on something proper to call him. Just been 'little man' for now."

Essence sucked her teeth. "Girl, not you out here on the run wit' a baby nicknamed that sounds like he selling loosies outside the corner store." But as she peered down, her expression melted. "Damn though, look at this child. He beautiful."

Bailey blinked back tears. "Got your lips," she whispered, finger hovering near the baby's face. "But those eyes..."

Shiffon shifted the bundle against her chest. "Let's not go there right now," she said voice clipped.

The apartment fell quiet except for the baby's soft breathing.

"We laid flowers on an empty casket," Leila said finally, voice cracking. "White roses. Your favorite."

"Had to be that way." Shiffon's apology came wrapped in steel. "Only way we both survive. If anyone thought I was breathing, this little man wouldn't be." She adjusted the blanket around his sleeping face.

Essence's gold bangles clinked as she folded her arms. "Since when we qualify as 'anyone'?"

"Since Genesis put money on my head," Shiffon answered, meeting Essence's glare with hollow eyes. "Since Maverick made enemies who'd hurt anything he loved just to wound him. Since I decided y'all deserved better than body bags for Christmas presents. Anybody I touched became collateral damage." She swallowed hard. "Couldn't risk y'all catching bullets meant for me. Anybody gettin' close to me was a target. Genesis had already put a kill order on my head. Maverick had enemies everywhere. I wasn't about to put y'all on the front line of some shit I wasn't sure I'd make it out of."

The mention of Genesis hung in the air like a curse.

Bailey shivered. "You heard what happened to him? You know he in the hospital, right?"

Shiffon's eyes hardened. "I heard. But a man like Genesis don't need to be conscious for his orders to keep breathin'." Her knees buckled slightly as she shifted the baby's weight. "Y'all mind if I...?" She gestured toward the couch with a slight wince.

"Shit, where my manners at?" Essence swept magazines and a throw blanket off the cushions with one fluid motion. "Sit before you fall. What you need? Tea? Wine?"

Shiffon sank into the couch, cradling the baby against her chest. "Just water," she said immediately. "Nothing else. I gotta stay sharp."

Bailey's fingers fluttered in the space between them, not quite touching either Shiffon or the baby. "When's the last time you ate something proper?"

"Yesterday morning," Shiffon murmured, her hollow cheeks suddenly more apparent. "But go easy. My stomach forgot what full feels like."

Leila disappeared into the kitchen, calling over her shoulder, "Leftover pasta coming up. Got some garlic bread I can throw in the oven too."

Leila vanished into the kitchen as Essence returned, water bottle in one hand, suspicion in her eyes. She perched on the chair arm opposite Shiffon.

"Let me get this straight. You resurrect yourself, appear with a whole child, and choose Atlanta, the one city guaranteed to get you killed. Make it make sense."

Shiffon twisted the cap off, gulping water like salvation. Her gaze traveled between her friends.

"Riot Mercer," she said finally. "Maverick's right hand. He's hunting ghosts. Word got back to him I might not be dead." Her voice dropped. "If he gets confirmation? He only stops hunting for one of two prizes."

"Being what?" Bailey leaned forward, her voice barely carried across the room.

Shiffon's palm settled over her son's chest, counting heartbeats like prayer beads.

"My corpse," she whispered. "Or Maverick's son."

The apartment fell silent except for Christmas songs drifting through the walls from down the hall. Then, footsteps in the corridor. Measured. Deliberate. Approaching.

Everyone went still. Three precise knocks followed, neither urgent nor casual.

Essence's fingers crept toward the drawer. Bailey's breath caught. Leila froze between rooms, dish towel dangling uselessly from her grip. Beneath Shiffon's ribs, her heart hammered a warning.

"Nobody moves," she commanded, her eyes suddenly winter-cold, the softness of motherhood crystallizing into something lethal. "Not until we know exactly who the fuck waiting on the other side of that door."

Chapter Three

RIOT IN THE WIND

The black Escalade rolled slow down Auburn Avenue like it was stalking the street itself. The winter wind whipped between buildings, tugging at loose Christmas banners and rattling the oversized candy-cane decorations taped to lamp posts. Atlanta was dressed up for the holidays, but under all the glitter and LED lights, nothing felt cheerful.

Inside the SUV, Riot Mercer sat back in the leather seat, one arm stretched across the headrest, the other gripping a half-burned blunt between tattooed fingers. Smoke curled around him, hazy and slow, swirling like a restless ghost that couldn't settle.

His phone buzzed. Another message from the

streets. Another whisper. Another confirmation. Somebody had seen her. Or someone who looked too
much like her.

Riot exhaled long, eyes narrowing through the
haze.

"Ain't no way that bitch ain't dead," he muttered,
but he didn't sound convinced. Maverick's death
had broken something inside him, fractured loyalty,
cracked sanity, snapped whatever moral thread he
once had. First, he loss his brother Cortez and now
Maverick, a man who believed in him more than his
own blood ever did. He'd been a demon before, but
now? He was drifting into a version of himself even he
didn't recognize.

"You good back there?" his right-hand man Vez
asked from the passenger seat, adjusting his gloves.
Big dude. Simple-minded. Loyal. Dangerous when
pointed in the right direction.

Riot flicked ash into the tray. "I'm good."

"You don't look good."

Riot leaned forward, tapping the phone against
the back of Vez's seat. "Read that."

Vez picked up the phone, squinted. "Says somebody saw a girl crossin' the border wit' a baby. They
say she looked like—"

"Finish the sentence," Riot said, eyes going cold.

Vez swallowed. "She looked like Shiffon."

Riot knocked his head back against the headrest,
jaw clenching. "That's the third sighting this week.

Third." He snapped his fingers. "When you hear somethin' once, it's a rumor. Twice, it's a maybe. Three times...?"

"It's truth," Vez muttered.

Riot grinned, but it wasn't a happy grin. It was sharp, jagged, the kind meant for nightmares. "Exactly."

He reached into his pocket, pulling out a picture. It was worn around the edges like he'd handled it too many times. Shiffon in a cropped hoodie, hair half-up, smirking at the camera like she knew she was trouble. Maverick had kept this picture tucked in his wallet. Riot kept it tucked in his revenge.

"Mav didn't go out like that for no reason," Riot said quietly, rolling the picture between his fingers. "Somebody helped put him in the ground. That bitch had ties to Genesis and that nigga Caleb. I bet she sold Maverick out."

Vez nodded slowly. "But if she is alive... why she stay hidden so long?"

"Because she got somethin' worth protectin'," Riot said.

He didn't want to say it out loud. He didn't want to speak the baby into existence. But he'd heard enough whispers, enough murmurs from the streets. Maverick's seed. A son. A living, breathing legacy.

"Turn here," Riot ordered suddenly. "Next left."

Vez flicked on the signal and turned into a quiet Eastside neighborhood. Older houses. Brick. Fenced yards. Christmas lights strung unevenly across porches. And a house Riot knew well, Shiffon's mother's place. Riot had driven by twice already that morning. But this time, he wasn't just looking. He was done watching shadows.

"Pull up slow," he said.

The SUV crawled to a stop in front of the house. A teenage boy, fifteen, maybe sixteen, was sweeping the porch, bundled in a hoodie and puffer vest. Shiffon's little brother. He looked older now. Taller. But still had that stubborn set to his jaw.

Vez cracked his knuckles. "You want me to—"

"No," Riot cut in, opening the door. "I'll talk."

The air was sharp, cold, biting at the skin. Riot stepped out, hood up, chains tucked under his shirt. He moved like a ghost, quiet on the sidewalk, boots crunching lightly in the thin frost. The boy looked up. And froze.

Riot lifted one hand casually. "Chill, lil' man. I just wanna talk."

The kid took one step back toward the door. "I don't know you."

"Yeah, you do," Riot said coolly. "You know my type. You know my look. You from Atlanta, you can read danger before it speak."

The boy swallowed. "You need to leave."

"You got a sister named Shiffon?" Riot asked bluntly.

The boy's face changed, split-second panic that gave him away. Riot stepped closer, slow, controlled.

"See...that reaction right there? That tells me everything I need to know."

The boy's hand gripped the doorknob. "She dead."

Riot smirked. "Is she?"

The porch door cracked open behind the boy. Shiffon's mother. Older now. Tired eyes. Defeated. That can happen when you lose a child. Robe tight around her waist. She stepped out, shielding her son with one arm.

"Back away from my house," she snapped. Her voice didn't shake.

Riot liked that. He respected nerve. He tilted his head. "You her mama."

"I said back away," she repeated.

"You know what I am?" Riot asked, leaning on the porch railing.

"Yes," she said. "And I'm not scared."

Riot's grin widened. "You should be."

Vez shifted behind him, hand near his waistband.

Shiffon's mother stepped forward. "My daughter is dead. But even if she was alive, I would die before I told you where she was."

The boy glanced up at her, fear mixing with pride.

Riot clicked his tongue. "See, you sayin' that? Nothin' but confirmation she alive." He tapped the side of his head. "'Cause a mother grieving a dead child ain't defiant. She broken."

Shiffon's mother's jaw tightened, but she didn't crack.

Riot stepped back off the porch. "You protect her then. Admire that." His eyes sharpened. "But if she come around here again? If she bring that baby around here...? I'll know." He turned to leave but paused. Then looked back at the boy. "You look like you'd fight for your sister," Riot said. "Don't make me test that."

The boy stood taller. "Don't make me fail."

Riot actually chuckled. "I like your spirit."

He turned and headed back to the SUV. Vez climbed in beside him. As the doors shut, Riot's smile vanished.

"She in the city," Riot said darkly. "And she bold enough to risk comin' home."

Vez nodded. "What you wanna do?"

Riot stared out the window as frost began crystallizing on the glass.

"Hunt," he said. "But slow. Like a storm. She won't see me 'til I'm already on her." He looked up at the sky. Snowflakes drifted down, lazy and soft. "A savage winter," Riot murmured. "Perfect time for death."

Chapter Four

A MOTHER'S HEART

By the time night fell, the snow had thickened into a soft, steady flurry, rare for Atlanta, the kind that made traffic slow down and folks post excited videos like they hadn't seen snow before. But for Shiffon, the winter air didn't feel magical or pretty. It felt like a countdown.

She paced the apartment quietly; her son nestled in her arms. Essence, Bailey, and Leila were pretending to watch a holiday movie on low volume, but nobody was paying attention. The tension in the room was thick enough to slice.

"You keep wearin' a hole in this floor," Essence finally muttered, sipping her wine without looking away from the screen.

"I'm fine," Shiffon lied.

"No, you're not." Leila glanced over. "You've been spooked since you walked in here. Now you have us spooked. To the point, we had guns raised for a knock at the door that turned out to be someone at the wrong apartment. They had no clue how close they came to having their head blown off," she sighed.

"My bad. My nerves are shot and my emotions are all over the place," Shiffon admitted.

Bailey shifted uneasily. "Is it...Genesis?"

Shiffon shook her head. "Not him. Not today." She swallowed hard. "I just...I need to see my mother."

Essence paused the TV. "Shiffon..."

"No." Shiffon held up one hand. "Y'all don't get it. She thought I died. They buried an empty casket. They cried over air. My baby's grandmother doesn't even know he exists." Her voice thickened, cracking around the edges. "I can't be in this city and not let her see he's real. She's literally only a few blocks away. I can't be this close and not see her."

Bailey stood. "We can take you."

"I can take myself," Shiffon said immediately.

Essence slid off the couch. "Sis, you just fled the fuckin' country with a newborn. There are people lookin' for you with guns and motivation. You ain't running around Atlanta alone."

Shiffon tightened her grip around her son. "I'll be careful. Real quick in and out. Ten minutes."

Leila squinted. "You already made up your mind, didn't you?"

Shiffon nodded.

Essence sighed. "Fine. But you takin' a burner phone, no rideshares, and you stay off main streets. And if you see anything suspicious? You turn yo' ass right back around."

"Deal," Shiffon whispered.

Bailey helped her bundle the baby, soft little hat, warm fleece suit, blanket tucked snug around him. He stared up with wide, curious eyes Shiffon desperately hoped wouldn't resemble Maverick's forever.

Essence handed her a black hoodie, a mask, and a small gun. "If Riot catches you alone—"

"He won't," Shiffon cut in. "But I appreciate the pep talk."

Essence smirked. "Bitch, I was being serious."

Shiffon's eyes softened. "I know."

With one more glance at the women she trusted more than she trusted herself, Shiffon slipped out into the cold.

○○○

Shiffon had to mentally prepare herself for her journey home. She didn't call a car. Didn't use the main roads. She walked, hood low, baby strapped tight, her steps soundless on the thin layer of snow gathering on the sidewalk.

The city felt muffled. Quiet. As if Atlanta itself was

holding its breath, waiting to see who would bleed first.

As she turned the corner onto her mother's street, her heart beat harder. Her childhood home came into view, the faded porch swing, the frost-dusted hydrangea bushes, the Christmas wreath that had been reused for six years straight. Shiffon froze. The porch light was on. The curtains were moving. And her mother, was sitting beside the window. Head in her hand. Staring out at the street like she had been waiting for weeks, months, years.

Shiffon's knees went weak.

She stepped into the yard, boots sinking into snow. Before she reached the porch, the front door opened. Her mother stood in the doorway, robe wrapped tight around her, breath trembling in the cold. For a heartbeat, they only stared.

Then the older woman whispered, "My baby?" like she didn't trust her own eyes.

Shiffon broke. "Ma..."

Her mother stumbled forward, arms out, fingers trembling as they brushed Shiffon's shoulder, her cheek, her hair, touching like she had to confirm this was flesh, not spirit.

"You're alive," her mother cried, pulling her into a fierce hug. "You're alive. Lord, thank you, my baby's alive."

Shiffon collapsed into her, one arm wrapped around her mother, the other steadying the baby between them. Tears burned hot down her cheeks despite the cold.

"I'm sorry," Shiffon whispered. "I'm so sorry."

Her mother cupped her face. "Baby, I don't care why you left. I don't care what happened. You here. That's all that matter."

Shiffon swiped tears quickly. "There's something I gotta show you." She turned the baby carrier toward her mother.

Her mother's hand flew to her mouth, eyes widening behind her tears. "Oh my God... Shiffon..."

Her brother came rushing out behind her mother, stopping in the doorway with shock freezing him mid-step. He wasn't little anymore. Shoulders broader. Voice deeper. But his eyes lit up like he was eleven again.

"Shiffon?" he whispered. "Shiffon!"

He ran down the stairs and hugged her so tightly she felt her ribs protest.

"This is your nephew," Shiffon said sweetly, lifting the blanket slightly.

Her mother touched the baby's tiny hand. "He's beautiful..." Her voice cracked again. "What's his name?"

Shiffon laughed weakly. "I haven't picked one yet."

Her mother smoothed the baby's cheek gently. "He already look like he know who he belong to."

Shiffon exhaled shakily. She hadn't felt this safe, this held, in months.

Her mother whispered, "You can stay. Both of you. At least for the night."

Shiffon's heart broke all over again. "Ma... I can't. It's not safe."

Her mother's expression shifted. "Who after you?"

Shiffon shook her head. "You don't want that answer."

Her brother tensed. "Shiffon...somebody came here earlier. A dude. Tall. Hood up. He... he asked about you."

Shiffon's blood went cold.

"When?" she whispered.

"A few hours ago." He looked tormented. "I didn't tell him nothin', I swear. But he looked like the type that don't give up easily when he diggin' for dirt."

Her mother closed her eyes. "He said somethin' about you... and a baby. I thought he was crazy. But you do have a baby."

Shiffon's breath caught in her throat. Riot. He had already been here. Already sniffing around the one place she should've never come. Shiffon forced herself to stand taller. Harden her voice. "I have to go. Now."

Her mother grabbed her arm. "No. You can't go back out there alone. That man...he had death in his eyes."

Shiffon swallowed hard. "Ma...you don't know the half of what he's capable of." She kissed her mother's cheek. "But I'll be okay. I always am."

Her brother clenched his jaw. "If he come back, I'm fightin' him."

Shiffon touched his face gently. "You better not. You hear me?" her eyes sharpened. "I can't lose you too."

Her mother watched her bundle the baby tighter and pull her hood up.

"Just tell me one thing," her mother said. "Is he tryna harm you and my grandson?"

Shiffon hesitated. Then nodded once.

Her mother's eyes glistened with the kind of anger only a mother could hold. "Then that man gon' get what's comin' to him."

Shiffon hugged her one last time, kissed her brother's forehead, and slipped back into the night.

The moment she reached the sidewalk, she saw it.

Two footprints in the snow. Large. Deep. Fresh. Leading toward her mother's house. Shiffon glanced down the street. Far away, half-hidden by a streetlamp flickering in the cold, a figure stood beside a dark SUV. Hood up. Watching the house. Watching her. Her spine went rigid.

Riot. He hadn't left the neighborhood. He was still lurking like a thirsty predator. Shiffon stepped backward slowly, her son held against her, heart hammering. She didn't run. Didn't panic. She simply turned, slipped between two houses, and disappeared into the darkness like she had never been there.

Chapter Five

THREE KINGS, THREE KILLERS

The morning after Shiffon's dangerous visit home, the apartment felt tight with unspoken fear. The snow outside had thickened into a glittering white sheet, turning the city into a postcard, beautiful, deceptive, hiding danger under every soft drift.

Shiffon barely slept. Essence definitely didn't. Leila and Bailey kept glancing out the windows like they expected Riot to materialize at any second. That's why when a new job came across their encrypted line, the three women damn near sighed with relief. They needed money. They needed distraction. And they needed something familiar to remind them they were still who they were. Killers. Assassins. Professionals.

Essence slid her phone onto the kitchen island. "Alright, listen up. Got a hit request."

Leila raised a brow. "Holiday hit? From who?"

"Client going by the name Frostbite," Essence said, rolling her eyes. "Probably some corny rich dude who thinks he edgy."

"What's the target?" Bailey asked, biting into a muffin.

Essence smirked. "Y'all gon' love this."

Shiffon rocked her baby gently as the women gathered around the phone.

Essence tapped the screen. A face filled the display.

Bailey gasped. Leila's jaw dropped. Shiffon blinked in disbelief.

"That's—" Bailey started.

"Yep," Essence confirmed. "Martina Luxe."

Martina Luxe. Instagram royalty. Twelve million followers. Known for luxury lifestyle reels, 'Boss Babe' quotes, expensive travel, and three-hour get-ready-with-me videos dripping in Chanel, Balmain, and fake vulnerability. She was the face of holiday campaigns, the star of beauty collabs, the queen of soft glam...And apparently, the mastermind behind half-a-dozen fake Christmas charities that stole money from thousands of followers every December.

"She scammed grandmothers, single moms, and

broke people tryna be generous for the holidays," Essence read. "Client claims she funneled hundreds of thousands into offshore accounts."

"Damn," Leila muttered. "Not Instagram fake holiday scams. Using Christmas to steal," she shook her head in dismay.

Bailey frowned. "So, what's the job? Scare her? Expose her?"

Essence scrolled. "Nah, baby. This a full hit." She tapped the screen again. "Client wants her dead before Christmas Eve."

Shiffon's baby cooed softly in the background as she made her way to the living room. She glanced over, watching the three women circle the kitchen island like wolves.

"Where the hit supposed to go down?" she asked.

Essence turned the screen around with a grin. "At her holiday charity gala."

Leila choked. "She got a charity gala while runnin' fake charities?"

"Hypocrisy at its finest," Essence said. "But get this, this gala? It's not some regular ballroom event." She zoomed in on the venue image. "She rented out an entire winter-themed private rooftop garden downtown. Snow machines. Ice sculptures. A Swarovski crystal tree. Champagne fountains."

Bailey let out a slow whistle. "Damn. That bitch living."

"More like dying," Essence corrected.

Leila cracked her knuckles. "Holiday outfits required, huh?"

Essence smirked. "Oh, you know it and of course the client will foot the bill. Frostbite said come glam. Blend into the influencer crowd. So, we're goin' all out. Fur coats. Heels. Sparkles. Whatever."

Bailey clasped her hands dramatically. "Fabolous baby!! I been waiting for an excuse to look like money I don't have."

They laughed, a brief moment of normalcy cutting through the tension of the last 24 hours. Shiffon watched them from the couch in silence. Her heart squeezed a little.

They needed this. They needed to feel like themselves again.

Essence turned to her. "Shiffon...we got this. I know you tempted to get back in the game, but you sit this one out. Focus on the baby."

Shiffon raised a brow. "Did you forget who taught y'all more than half the tricks you know?"

Leila walked over and bent down to adjust the baby's blanket. "Girl, we didn't forget. But until Riot is handled, your only job is keepin' him alive." She touched the baby's hand gently. "He needs you more than anything we got going on."

Bailey grabbed her sparkly purse off the counter. "We'll be in and out. Quick and clean."

Shiffon nodded. She hated sitting out. Hated feeling like prey. But they weren't wrong. Her son was everything now, and danger moved differently when you had something to lose.

"Wear the white fur coat," Shiffon said, voice steady. "It makes you look harmless and rich. And put a wire blade inside the clutch."

Essence smirked. "See? Knew you couldn't resist giving orders."

Bailey winked. "We'll bring you back a souvenir."

Leila grabbed her gun. "Preferably one of Martina's wigs."

Essence checked the time. "Alright, baddies. Christmas assassination. Let's go.

○○○

Martina Luxe's rooftop gala event was everything an influencer's dreams were made of, and everything a normal person should avoid. Artificial snow drifted through the air, glistening under chandeliers shaped like frosted stars. A Swarovski-encrusted runway led to a giant tree dripping in diamonds and silver ornaments. The champagne fountain sparkled. Photographers snapped nonstop. Soft jazz versions of trap songs played in the background.

Essence, Bailey, and Leila stepped onto the rooftop in slow motion, coats gleaming, makeup flawless, eyes cold and calculating. Heads turned. Phones lifted. Flashes popped. Because they looked expensive. They looked dangerous. They looked like they belonged.

Bailey leaned close. "This is giving Bougie Mission Impossible vibes."

Essence scanned the crowd. "Where the target?"

Leila spotted her first. Martina Luxe stood near the tree, laughing into her champagne, wearing a gown that probably cost more than Essence's first car. Her smile was wide. Her followers adored her. Cameras loved her. But Essence saw something else. The arrogance. The entitlement. The greed.

"Target acquired," Essence murmured. "Time to—"

Her earpiece crackled.

A voice she did NOT expect came through. "Abort."

Essence froze. Bailey blinked. Leila whipped around.

The voice repeated, sharper this time.

"I said abort the hit."

Essence whispered, "Shiffon? What the—?"

But she already knew. Because standing behind the chocolate fountain, half-hidden in blue lighting, wearing a long black coat and a hood pulled low...Was Shiffon. With her gun drawn. Eyes locked on a man across the rooftop. A man pointing a weapon at Martina Luxe. Not a hired assassin. Not a rival influencer. Not a random threat.

A man working for Riot Mercer.

Shiffon didn't look at them. Didn't blink. Didn't breathe.

"Riot sent someone to kill the target first," Shiffon whispered into the earpiece. "Which means this job? This bitch? This gala? It's a setup."

Leila's blood ran cold. "Meaning...?"

Shiffon stepped out from behind the fountain, weapon steady. "Meaning Riot is using Martina's death as bait to smoke us out. And he's close. Really close."

The snow machines kicked up just then, blasting glittering flakes across the rooftop. Essence drew her gun.

Bailey lifted her champagne flute like nothing was wrong.

Leila slid her blade from its clutch. And Shiffon moved toward the shooter with the silent, graceful confidence of a woman who'd once been the deadliest thing in any room. Even motherhood couldn't dim that. She was still

Shiffon. Still lethal. Still the baddest assassin breathing. And tonight, Riot was going to learn that the hard way.

Chapter Six

JINGLE BELLS & GUN SHELLS

Artificial snow drifted across the rooftop as if the night were enchanted, glamorous, magical, until the first gunshot cracked through the holiday jazz. Shiffon fired first. Her bullet sliced clean through the air, knocking the shooter's weapon out of his hand before he could line up his aim again. Martina Luxe screamed, stumbling backward into the Swarovski tree as the rooftop erupted into chaos, heels slipping, champagne flutes shattering, influencers shrieking like horror-movie extras.

Essence snapped into action instantly. "Bailey,

crowd control, move 'em left! Leila, you're with me!"

Bailey lifted her champagne glass like she was still partying, her voice a sugary scream that matched the panic around them. "OMG, ACTIVE SHOOTER! EVERY-BODY RUN THIS WAY! THIS WAY, Y'ALL!!" She herded people toward the far exit with frightening efficiency, panic management was a special kind of skill.

Leila slid through the chaos, blade hidden in her clutch, eyes locked on the shooter who was scrambling to grab his weapon from the ground. Too slow. Shiffon was already there. She kicked the gun further away, heel digging into the rooftop tiles as she stared down the man sent to kill both Martina and her crew.

He looked up at her, nose bleeding, fury twisting his features. "Bitch... you—"

Shiffon cut him off with a brutal strike to the jaw. "Don't talk."

Leila whistled low. "Ooooh, she back."

Essence appeared beside them, gun steady in her hand. "Tie him."

Shiffon grabbed the shooter by the collar and dragged him behind a decorative snowman as partygoers trampled toward the emergency stairs. The rooftop lights flickered under the sudden strain of bodies stampeding.

The shooter spat blood. "Riot gon'—"

Shiffon pistol-whipped him so fast Leila didn't even blink. "I said don't talk."

Essence smirked. "Damn, I missed you."

Bailey rushed back over, breathing hard. "The rooftop's almost clear. Security's coming. We gotta move now."

But Leila wasn't looking at the shooter anymore. She was scanning the rooftop perimeter, the trees, the glass walls, the balcony, the shadows cast by twinkling lights. Her face shifted.

"Shiffon," she whispered. "We got a problem."

Shiffon followed Leila's gaze. A tall figure stood on the building across from them. Black coat. Gloved hands. Mask covering the lower half of his face. Watching. Not hiding. Not running. Watching. Motherhood had sharpened Shiffon's instincts, not dulled them. Her breath caught. Riot.

He stepped forward into the faint glow of a rooftop security light. Then he lifted his hands. Not to wave. Not to aim a weapon. He made a cradle shape with his arms, curving them gently, palms up, and rocked them slowly, deliberately. Like he was holding a baby. *Her* baby. Shiffon's blood turned to ice.

He wasn't pointing in any direction. He wasn't gesturing toward anyone present. He was sending a message: *I know. I know you had a child. I know he exists. And I'm coming for him.*

Essence's voice crackled through the earpiece, frantic.

"Shiffon! You froze. What is it? You see somebody?"

Bailey appeared beside her, face pale. "Who are you lookin' at?"

39

Shiffon couldn't speak yet. Because Riot wasn't done.

He finished the rocking motion, then lifted one finger, and pressed it to his lips. ***Shhh. Don't let them hear him cry. Or I'll find him faster.***

Shiffon staggered back a step, fury and terror crashing like thunder in her chest. Essence climbed onto a decorative bench to see what Shiffon was staring at.

Her heart dropped. "Don't let it be that muthafucker," she whispered. "Is that—?"

"Riot," Shiffon choked out. "He knows. He knows about my son."

And then Riot disappeared, stepping back into the shadows as if the rooftop swallowed him whole.

Shiffon grabbed the shooter by the face, fury trembling in her voice. "What did he tell you to do tonight? Huh? WHAT WAS THE PLAN?"

The man laughed, even with a split lip. "Riot wanted the Bad Bitches Only crew on a rooftop under bright lights, out in the open, distracted...while he watched Shiffon's reactions and confirmed the rumor he'd been chasing across borders: She had a baby.

Bailey's stomach dropped. "Meaning he wasn't tryna kill Martina just to kill her. He was—"

"Flushing us out," Shiffon finished, jaw tight. "This entire hit was bait."

Essence looked around the glittering destruction of the rooftop. "And we walked right into it."

Leila knelt beside the shooter. "Did Riot tell you to kill us too?"

The shooter smiled through blood. "Kill? Nah. He said Shiffon gotta stay alive... at least long enough to give the boy over."

Shiffon's pulse roared in her ears. She wanted to shoot the man, kill him right there, send Riot a message, but no. A dead messenger told no stories. A live one lied too much. She leaned close instead.

"You go back to Riot," she uttered, "and you tell him this: if he ever gets close to my son... I'll show him what it means to die slow."

The shooter's grin faltered.

Essence grabbed the man by the collar. "Should we drop him off the roof? Blame it on the ice?"

Bailey raised her hand. "I volunteer to push."

Shiffon shook her head. "We don't have time. Take his phone. His wallet. Anything traceable. Then leave him."

Leila blinked. "Leave him?"

"Alive," Shiffon clarified. "I want Riot to know exactly how close I got."

"And how close he didn't," Essence added with a mean smile.

Sirens began wailing below. Spotlights swung across the rooftop from a helicopter, catching the glitter of fake snow and broken champagne glasses.

Bailey tugged Shiffon's elbow. "We gotta go. Now."

Leila was already moving toward the exit. "Emergency stairs. Down two levels. Then out the back alley."

Essence rolled her eyes. "This bitch got blueprints memorized."

"Would you prefer we get arrested on a rooftop while wearing sequins?" Leila shot back.

Essence grinned. "Actually... good point."

They moved fast, heels clacking, glitter swirling behind them like fairy dust from hell. Shiffon kept to the rear, her gun tucked close, every nerve in her body screaming to get back to her son immediately.

When they burst out into the alleyway behind the building, the snow hit them like a curtain. Cold, biting, thick enough to coat the ground in minutes. A message was spray-painted on the side wall in dripping black paint that hadn't been there before: ***BRING ME THE BABY. — R***

Bailey's hand flew to her mouth. "This nigga is relentless."

Leila shivered. "He was here. Like... minutes ago."

Essence's voice dropped. "Shiffon...this man is obsessed."

Shiffon stared at the message, her breath fogging in the cold air. "No," she whispered. "He's desperate." She turned away, snowflakes catching on her lashes as her voice hardened into ice. "And desperate men are the easiest ones to kill."

Chapter Seven

SILENT NIGHT AT THE SAFE HOUSE

The snow was falling harder now—fat, heavy flakes that coated the windshield as Bailey sped through the back streets of Midtown. The city blurred past in white streaks and Christmas lights. Sirens wailed faintly in the distance, fading behind them as they ducked into smaller and smaller roads. They'd stopped just long enough for Shiffon to scoop up her sleeping son from Essence's cousin's apartment, tucking him safely into the car before making a beeline for the safe house. Shiffon held him tight now, every bump of the road reminding her how close Riot had come to finding out the truth she wasn't ready for him to see.

"Make three more turns. I don't want nobody trailing us," Essence directed.

Bailey's jaw tightened. "I already made five. This is some Fast & Furious shit."

"Insequins," Leila muttered, pulling off her lashes in the back seat. "This is what we get for trying to kill somebody at a Christmas pageant."

Shiffon hadn't said a word since they left the gala. She stared out the side window, chest rising and falling too fast. Snowflakes melted on her heated skin the second they landed, her fingers twitching like she wanted a weapon in her hand. Not because of the shooter. Not because of the setup. Because Riot had made a cradle gesture on a rooftop and told her without saying a word: I know your son exists. And I'm coming. To Shiffon he had declared war.

Bailey turned down a narrow alley, killed the headlights, and eased into the side garage of an abandoned short-term rental Shiffon had used years ago for jobs.

"Alright," Bailey exhaled, "we're here."

The women piled out quickly, heels clacking on the cracked pavement. Shiffon moved first, practically sprinting toward the door. Essence unlocked it, ushering everyone inside. Leila flicked on a single lamp, soft yellow light spilling across dusty furniture. Finally safe-ish. Finally able to breathe. But Shiffon didn't breathe. She paced. Essence shut the door, clicked all three locks, then slid down the wall, adrenaline still bleeding from her skin.

"Alright," she said, voice sharp, "what the entire fuck happened tonight?"

Everything spilled out at once.

Bailey: "The shooter was on the payroll—"

Leila: "Riot's payroll—"

Essence: "He was WATCHING the rooftop."

Bailey: "He made a baby-rockin' motion at Shiffon!"

Leila: "Which is creepy as hell, by the way."

Shiffon finally stopped pacing. Her voice was low, dark. "There is no more guessing. He for sure knows about my son." That was the only thing on her mind.

Silence. Cold. Heavy.

Essence rubbed her temples. "Okay. Let's break this down from the top. First off, how the hell did you even know the job was fake? How you know Frostbite wasn't a real client?"

All eyes snapped to Shiffon.

She sat down slowly, hands shaking, rubbing them together like she could scrub off the fear.

"Because the minute y'all left," she began, "I felt something was off."

"What you mean?" Leila asked.

Shiffon inhaled deeply. "Assassin gigs have rhythms. Patterns. Certain signatures in the communication. And little things ain't add up, so I checked."

Essence leaned forward. "Checked what?"

"Everything," Shiffon said. "First? The client profile."

She ticked points off on her fingers: "Account was made yesterday. No history. Payment wired too fast. No negotiation. No clarification. No questions."

Leila frowned. "Damn. That IS suspicious."

"Then," Shiffon continued, "I traced the payment trail."

"That quick?" Bailey blinked.

Shiffon shot her a look. "Motherhood didn't make me stupid."

Essence snorted. "Tell 'em."

"So," Shiffon said, voice calm but fire beneath it, "the deposit was sent through a masked crypto string bouncing between three wallets...but the tagging pattern? The fingerprint?" she shook her head. "I recognized it."

Leila sat back slowly. "Riot."

Shiffon nodded. "He used that exact same pattern when Maverick made him handle offshore money." Her lip curled. "He sloppy and thinks hiding behind a VPN makes him invisible."

Bailey's eyes widened. "So, you knew right then?"

"That told me something was wrong," Shiffon said. "But what confirmed it was the gala itself."

Essence frowned. "The gala?"

"Yeah." Shiffon pulled out her phone and swiped open Instagram. "I went on social media. Looked up Martina Luxe's live stories. Guests were posting all night. Champagne. Flowers. Snow machines. Influencer bullshit."

"Facts," Bailey muttered.

Shiffon tapped one of the videos. "And then I saw him."

Essence leaned in. "Saw who?"

Shiffon zoomed in on a frame, a man holding up a drink behind Martina Luxe. On his knuckles? A sharp, geometric tattoo. Distinct. Hard to forget.

"That's one of Riot's foot soldiers," Shiffon said. "He worked for Maverick before. I spotted him instantly."

Bailey's mouth dropped. "Ohhhh shit."

Leila shook her head slowly. "So, the hit wasn't a hit. It was bait."

"Exactly," Shiffon said. "Riot wanted y'all on that rooftop. He wanted me to panic, track y'all, show up. He needed proof I was alive, and that the baby exists."

Essence's voice shook. "So, he ain't after us."

"No," Shiffon whispered. "He's after my son."

Silence again. But this time it wasn't fear. It was rage.

Leila stood, fists clenched. "We can't stay here."

Bailey nodded. "We gotta move every few hours."

Essence crossed her arms. "And we need to prepare for the fact Riot is not gon' stop."

Shiffon finally sat still. The lamp beside her flickered once. Snow whispered against the cracked window. Her son slept in the small portable bassinet Bailey had set up earlier. And Shiffon whispered the truth they were all too scared to say aloud:

"He crossed a line tonight. He threatened my child. And I don't care if it's Christmas, winter, or Judgment Day... if Riot wants a war?" she lifted her head, eyes like flint. "He gon' get one."

Chapter Eight

MARKET OF MIRACLES & MONSTERS

The safe house felt like a pressure cooker. Too quiet. Too still. Too easy for fear to ferment. By morning, the snow had stopped, but the sky still hung low and gray, like winter was waiting to pounce again. Shiffon fed her son in the dim bedroom while Essence brewed coffee so strong it could strip paint. Bailey paced the kitchen, checking through the blinds every three minutes. Leila sat at the table sharpening a blade she claimed was "for emotional support."

By noon, Shiffon's nerves were frayed.

"We need supplies," she said, bouncing her son

gently. "Formula, diapers, wipes, batteries... y'all forget newborns burn through shit quick."

Essence lifted a brow. "You tryin' to go outside after last night?"

"No," Shiffon snapped, then forced her voice calmer. "Not alone."

Essence sighed. "I'll go with you."

Bailey started to push up from the chair. "I'll go too."

"Stay," Shiffon said quickly. "One of us has to be with my son. If Riot makes a move... I need y'all here."

Bailey's eyes softened, and she sat back down.

Leila nodded. "We'll guard him."

Essence tossed her braids back. "Alright then. Let's move."

Shiffon strapped on a small knife under her hoodie, tucked a pistol into her waistband, and kissed her sleeping son's forehead.

Essence locked the door behind them. "This is a quick run. In and out. No extra stops."

Shiffon smirked tiredly. "You talking to me like I'm the one who takes detours for croissants."

"Girl, hush." Essence rolled her eyes. "Stay close."

◯◯◯

The Little Five Points holiday market was packed, wall-to-wall people in puffer coats and ugly Christmas sweaters, kids tugging parents toward hot cocoa carts, couples taking selfies under rainbow-lit snowflakes strung between trees. Handmade ornaments, candles, spiced cider... Atlanta had turned a quirky neighborhood into a winter fairytale.

Perfect place to blend in. Perfect place to disappear.

Perfect place for an ambush. Essence kept her hand tucked inside her coat, gripping the handle of a weapon nobody could see.

"Grab formula first," Shiffon muttered. "Then diapers. Then we gone."

Shiffon's eyes scanned every corner, every vendor, every cluster of people. The air smelled like cinnamon and woodsmoke, but beneath it, she could taste danger. They reached the pop-up convenience stand. Shiffon grabbed what she needed quickly, two cans of formula, wipes, travel bottles, even a teething toy shaped like a snowman.

Her fingers froze on the packaging, thinking of the last time she bought toys? She'd still believed she might get to raise her son somewhere safe.

Essence nudged her. "Focus."

"Yeah," Shiffon said, shaking herself. "Let's pay and go." But as she turned toward the register...A woman lifted her phone. Aiming it. Right at Shiffon. For a split second, Shiffon's heart slammed. She shifted her body sideways, face turned away.

Essence stiffened. "Is she recording us?"

The woman giggled to her friend. "No trying to get a pic of that Santa behind y'all. He got on Dior sneakers!"

Essence sneered. "Atlanta stay embarrassing."

Shiffon exhaled slowly. Her nerves were shot. She needed to get away from the crowd.

They paid and stepped back into the flow of people.

"Let's take the side alley," Essence said. "Less eyes."

They turned the corner, and Shiffon froze mid-step.

A tall, broad man stood near a vendor booth selling handmade wreaths. Black hoodie. Black jeans. Hands in pockets. Nothing unusual... except he wasn't looking at the wreaths. He was looking at Shiffon. Straight at her.

Essence murmured, "You see him?"

"Yeah." Shiffon kept walking, tone icy. "Don't make eye contact. Don't approach."

"He one of Riot's?" Essence asked under her breath.

"Maybe. Maybe not." Shiffon didn't blink. "But he's watching." They didn't speed up. Didn't run. Didn't draw attention. They walked like two women enjoying the holiday market on a winter afternoon. But the man followed. Slow. Measured. Never getting too close.

Essence's voice was low. "We need to lose him."

"Not here," Shiffon said. "Too many civilians. If he grabs for a gun and misses, somebody's child is getting hit."

Essence nodded. "Then where?"

Shiffon scanned the bustling crowd, the food stalls, the vendors, and then she saw it. An alley between two artisan shops. Narrow. Less foot traffic. A blind corner.

Perfect. She whispered, "Follow my lead."

They drifted toward the alley like they were browsing handmade soaps. The man followed. Predictable. Confident. As soon as they turned the corner, Shiffon grabbed Essence's arm.

"Three... two... now."

They swung into the shadows. Essence hit the wall and spun, gun raised. Shiffon lunged low, grabbing the first thing she could. a broken wooden pallet and shifted her grip like a blade. The man appeared at the opening of the alley.

Shiffon's voice dropped to ice. "Keep coming. I dare you." He stepped forward once.

Essence tightened her trigger finger. "Try it."

Shiffon didn't blink. "You want me? You want the baby? Or you just running errands for your boss?"

The man stopped. Then his face changed. Not fear. Not confusion. Recognition.

"Shiffon," he said. "I'm not here to hurt you."

Essence barked out a laugh. "Boy, shut the hell up."

The man raised empty hands. "My name's Calvin. Riot sent me—"

Shiffon lunged forward with frightening speed, slamming him into the wall. Formula cans clattered to the ground.

"You got exactly three seconds to explain," she snarled.

"I—I'm supposed to give you a message." He kept his hands up. "That's it."

Essence stepped closer. "Say it. And don't stutter."

The man swallowed. "Riot said to tell you... that the gala was just a warm-up."

Shiffon's lip curled. "What's the real message?"

Calvin hesitated. Eyes darted. Fear creeping up his neck. "He said—" His voice dropped. "—you know what he wants." He eyed both women before continuing. "And there's more." A cold gust swept through the alley.

Essence's eyes widened. "Spill it before I empty my clip on you."

Calvin's voice trembled. "He said... 'She knows what I want... so she knows what I'll take.'"

Shiffon's entire body went still. Because she did know. Because Riot had made it clear on that rooftop. He wasn't after her. He wasn't after the crew. He didn't care about the hit. He wanted her baby.

Essence's rage surged. "We should kill him."

"No," Shiffon said softly. Calvin sighed in relief, until she stepped closer, voice lethal.

"You go back to Riot and tell him this: I'm not surrendering my son. Not today. Not tomorrow. Not ever."

Essence added, "And tell him the next time we see your face, it won't be this friendly."

Calvin nodded quickly, scrambling away down the alley.

Essence grabbed Shiffon's arm. "I can't believe Riot sent that scarry actin' nigga to deliver his baby stealing message," she shook her head. "But we need to go. Now."

Shiffon scooped up the formula, breathing hard. "We're moving safe houses tonight," she said. "And we don't stop moving until Riot is six feet under."

Essence nodded. "I'm with you."

Shiffon's voice dropped to a whisper. No longer fear. No longer shock. Just pure, distilled wrath. "He wants my son?" She tightened her grip on the bag. "Then I want him dead."

Chapter Nine

SNOWFALL & SMOKE

Snow swallowed Atlanta in silence. Not the pretty, Christmas-card kind. The kind that muted sound, blurred edges, and made danger easier to hide. By late afternoon, the storm had thickened into a heavy white curtain. Streets were sparse, cars crawling, the city moving like someone had pressed slow motion. Shiffon stood at the edge of the safe house window, holding her son against her chest as he slept, his small breaths warming the hollow of her collarbone.

Bailey paced behind her, chewing a thumbnail. "This storm is wild. I ain't never seen Atlanta look like this."

Leila cracked her knuckles. "Nature doing vibes.

Riot doing violence. Great combo."

Essence was cleaning her gun with mechanical precision, jaw tight, movements clipped. "Riot gon' use this snow to move. Storms make men like him bold."

Shiffon didn't turn away from the window. "He already bold. The storm just make him reckless."

She couldn't stop replaying the alley encounter in her mind, the message, the fear in the messenger's eyes, the lie Riot was telling himself. He'd convinced himself he had a claim on her son. Like Maverick's death handed him a legacy he never earned. Not on her watch.

Leila wiped her hands on a towel. "Alright. Let's check the plan again. We move safe houses every twelve hours, different routes, no digital footprint—"

Her words cut off when Essence's phone buzzed.

Normally, Essence would ignore it. Nobody should be calling during a lockdown. But the name on the screen made her inhale sharply.

"Oh no," Essence whispered. "Y'all... it's my cousin."

Bailey's spine went stiff. "The one who babysits?"

Essence nodded. Hard.

Shiffon's heart dropped. "Answer it. Put it on speaker."

Essence's thumb shook as she tapped the screen. "Hello? Kendra?"

Static. Then a shaking voice.

"Essence... somebody... somebody banged on the door."

Shiffon felt her knees weaken. Her son stirred against her chest, sensing her fear.

Essence moved closer to the phone. "What? Who?!"

"I don't...I don't know," Kendra whispered. "A man. Tall. He pounded on the door and yelled that he needed to ask questions. He said someone told him I lived alone. He asked if I ever babysit."

Leila cursed low. "That was Riot's scout."

"Kendra, are you safe?" Shiffon demanded, voice cold with fear.

"Yeah, yeah," she breathed. "I didn't open the door. I didn't answer. I just grabbed the knife from the kitchen and got quiet. After a minute, he left."

Essence let out a breath she'd been holding. "Keep all doors locked. Leave a light on. Don't answer for no-body. We'll call you when it's safe."

Kendra's voice broke. "Essence... who did you bring around me?"

Essence swallowed tears. "Nobody. I swear. Just... just sit tight."

She ended the call, shoulders shaking. Leila rubbed her back. "You didn't do anything wrong."

Bailey nodded. "This is Riot. Not you."

Shiffon tightened her hold on her son, rage igniting inside her like a match dropped in gasoline. He was circling them. Testing boundaries. Tapping fences. Her baby whimpered, and she kissed the top of his head. "Shhh, little man. Mama got you."

Essence stood abruptly. "Alright. We're not waiting for him to make the next move."

Leila smirked. "Finally, some action."

But Shiffon turned away from the window, eyes glowing with something darker.

"No," she said. "We don't react today."

Essence blinked. "Sis... he came to my cousin's house."

"And that's why we don't react," Shiffon said. "That's what he wants."

Essence narrowed her eyes. "Explain."

Shiffon adjusted her son to her other shoulder. "Men like Riot crave chaos. He wants us flailing. Running. Making mistakes. But I know his type better than he think."

Leila crossed her arms. "Meaning?"

"Meaning," Shiffon said slowly, "he gets sloppy when he's sure he's winning."

Essence's lips parted. "So, we wait until he sloppy."

Shiffon nodded. "Exactly."

Then—A sound. Sharp. Distinct. Impossible to ignore. A scream. Not from inside. Outside. Bailey snapped to the window. "What the—?"

Leila yanked the blinds. "Whoa."

Down below, in the snowy street, a woman stood beside a Christmas market cart that had slid backward in the slush. A man was shouting at her, grabbing her wrist, towering over her dramatically. But that wasn't the problem. The problem was who the shouting man was.

Essence's voice dropped to a whisper. "Oh... hell."

Shiffon stepped forward, heart pounding. Standing in the middle of the snow-covered street, beneath flickering holiday lights, screaming at a random woman, was Riot Mercer. Not hiding. Not stalking. Not lurking in the shadows tonight. He was out in broad daylight, in the open, like a wolf that had finally stopped pretending to stalk. Leila cursed under her breath. "Why is he doing this out here?"

Essence's jaw clenched. "He wants eyes on him. He wants us to watch."

Riot yanked the woman's wrist once more, and she smacked him across the face. The slap cracked through the air. Riot froze. Turned his head slowly. And smiled. Dangerously.

Shiffon sighed, "Oh no." Because she knew that look. Too well. Riot grabbed the street vendor's entire Christmas cart and shoved it so hard it crashed into a parked car, ornaments exploding like gunfire. People screamed. Phones came out. Cameras flashed.

Riot stood in the falling snow, chest rising and falling, hands shaking like a man who had finally snapped.

Essence whispered, "He's unraveling."

"No," Shiffon corrected, her voice like ice. "He's escalating."

Riot turned, not toward the crowd, not toward the

woman, but toward their building. His eyes lifted and locked onto their window. Bailey gasped. Leila stumbled back. Essence raised her gun on instinct. And Shiffon? She stepped right up to the glass and stared him down. Snow fell between them. Smoke from the wrecked Christmas cart curled at Riot's feet. The distance didn't matter. He smiled at her. Slow. Predictable.

He mouthed two words: *"**YOUR TURN.**"*

Shiffon's breath left her chest in one violent rush. Because she knew exactly what that meant. Tonight... Riot wasn't just hunting. He was coming.

Chapter Ten

STORM WARNING

The power flickered once, twice, then held. For now.

The safe house creaked under the weight of the storm, wind rattling the windows like impatient fingers. Snow piled against the doorframes, sealing them in. Outside, sirens wailed somewhere far off, then vanished, swallowed by white. Shiffon closed the blinds herself. Slow. Deliberate. As if she could shut Riot out by force of will.

Bailey locked the deadbolt again even though it was already locked. "He saw us," she said quietly. "Like... really saw us."

Essence stood in the middle of the living room, phone pressed to her ear, listening to nothing but dead air. "Cell service is trash. Wi-Fi's hanging on by a prayer."

Leila checked the windows one by one, peering through slivers. "He's testing response time. Police. Neighbors. Us."

Shiffon lowered herself onto the couch with her son, easing him into the crook of her arm. His eyes fluttered open, dark and curious, unaware that a monster had just smiled at his mother through glass.

She smoothed a thumb across his cheek. "You okay, little man?"

He answered with a soft grunt and curled his fingers around her shirt.

Essence finally lowered the phone. "He wanted you to see him," she said. "That wasn't accidental."

"I know," Shiffon replied. Her voice was steady now, too steady. "He wanted to make sure I knew he's done hiding."

Bailey swallowed. "What happens next?"

Shiffon looked up at them. At all three of them. Sisters. Soldiers. Family. "What happens next," she said, "is he tightens the circle."

Leila leaned against the wall. "Dive deeper 'cause I'm not understanding."

"He'll apply pressure where he thinks I'm weakest," Shiffon said. "Friends. Family. Anyone he thinks I'll run toward."

Leila's jaw hardened. "He already sniffed around Essence's cousin."

"And my mother," Shiffon added softly. "He went to her house again yesterday."

Silence slammed into the room.

Bailey's eyes widened. "He what?"

Shiffon nodded once. "Didn't touch her. Didn't threaten her outright. Just... trying to instill fear, while interrogating. Her mouth twisted. "That's how men like him confirm things."

Leila cursed under her breath. "So, what do we do?"

Shiffon took a breath she'd been holding for months.

"We stop pretending I can outrun this," she said. "And I tell y'all the rest."

Essence's eyes narrowed. "The rest of what?"

Shiffon glanced down at her son. At the small rise and fall of his chest. Then she looked back up, resolve settling in her bones.

"Maverick's death," she said. "And how I got out."

Shiffon took a breath that felt like it came from somewhere deep in her bones. "The night everything went wrong... I wasn't running," she said quietly. "I was healing."

Essence frowned. "Healing from what?"

"I'd been shot," Shiffon replied. "Hospitalized. Maverick knew I was pregnant before he ever died. He knew the baby was his." Her jaw tightened. "And that's when everything around us started collapsing."

Bailey's eyes widened. "So, Maverick knew before

Genesis did."

"Yes," Shiffon said. "But Genesis found out anyway."

She shifted her son gently, grounding herself in the weight of him. "After Maverick kidnapped Amir... and Aaliyah and Angel... he learned through Caleb that I was pregnant. That the child I was carrying belonged to Maverick." Her voice dropped. "That made me leverage."

Now Essence and Bailey were cursing under their breath too.

"Genesis tried to trade me," Shiffon continued. "Me and my unborn child... for Amir."

Essence went still. "That's sick."

"It gets worse," Shiffon said. "There was supposed to be an exchange. But before it could happen, Genesis learned the truth." Her throat tightened. "Amir was already dead."

Silence slammed into the room.

"That's when Genesis snapped," Shiffon said. "He ordered Caleb to kill me. Not business. Not strategy. Revenge."

Bailey whispered, "That's why everyone thought you were dead."

Shiffon nodded. "Because that's what Caleb told him. That rumor soon spread through the streets." She looked up, eyes sharp but grateful. "As you can see, Caleb didn't kill me. He protected me. He hid me until I gave birth. Then he gave me a new identity and sent me out of the country with my son." Her voice cracked just slightly. "He saved our lives. And now, I put our lives in jeopardy by coming back."

Leila leaned forward slowly. "So, Genesis believes you're dead."

"Yes," Shiffon said. "Everyone did until I came back."

Essence frowned. "So, who killed Maverick?"

"From what I was told, Genesis killed Maverick himself. Shot him. Ended it." Her gaze hardened. "

She looked down at her son, brushing her thumb across his cheek. "With me and Maverick both being dead, they all thought the past was buried," she said softly. "But you don't bury something like this without consequences."

The wind rattled the windows again, as if the city itself agreed. "And now," Shiffon finished, "Riot knows the truth. That Maverick has a son. And he thinks that gives him a claim." Her eyes lifted, burning. "It doesn't. After Maverick's death, Riot isn't mourning like a normal man. He's looking for ownership."

Leila scoffed. "Yep, he seems to believe your son is his inheritance..."

Shiffon finished. "Or his leverage."

Essence slammed her palm against the counter. "Over my dead body."

A sudden gust rattled the windows harder this time. The lights dimmed, then snapped back.

Shiffon stood. "He wants to force me into a mistake," she said. "To run. To panic. To expose my son."

Leila stepped forward. "So, we don't give him that."

"No," Shiffon agreed. "We flip it."

Bailey blinked. "Flip it how?"

Shiffon walked to the table, spreading out the city map Bailey had printed earlier. She traced a finger through neighborhoods, streets, access points.

"He's escalating publicly," she said. "Which means he's feeling pressure. Which means his resources are stretched."

Essence's eyes lit. "You think we can bait him."

"I know we can," Shiffon said.

Leila smiled slowly. "Oh. I like this version."

"But not tonight," Shiffon added. "Tonight, we fortify. We disappear again."

She looked back at her son, then at the women who'd chosen to stand with her.

"And tomorrow," she said, voice steel, "we remind Riot Mercer that storms cut both ways."

Beyond their walls, the storm intensified, each gust flinging ice crystals against windows like scattered bullets. The calendar might say December, but this wasn't just winter's bite—it was nature mirroring their reality. Shiffon felt it in her bones: Tonight, Riot had stopped circling, he'd chosen his moment to strike and they were ready to strike back.

Chapter Eleven

CHRISTMAS EVE AMBUSH

Christmas Eve arrived wrapped in silence. Not the peaceful kind. The waiting kind. The storm had eased just enough to make people believe the worst had passed. Snow still coated the streets, but plows had carved narrow paths through it. Lights flickered back on across the city. Radios played carols like nothing was wrong. Inside the safe house, nobody trusted the calm.

Shiffon stood in the hallway tightening the strap of the baby carrier, testing it twice. Her son slept against her chest, warm and steady. She'd wrapped him in layers, soft, quiet fabrics that wouldn't rustle if she moved fast. Essence checked the back door. Bailey checked the windows. Leila checked the traps. They hadn't decorated. No tree. No stockings. Just weapons laid out neatly on the dining table like offerings.

"This place is too obvious," Leila muttered, adjusting a thin wire stretched low across the kitchen doorway. "He's gonna come."

Essence nodded. "Tonight."

Shiffon didn't argue. She already felt it, an itch under her skin, the same one she used to get before a hit went bad.

"He wants Christmas," she said quietly. "Symbolic. Public fear. He's dramatic like that."

Bailey exhaled. "Of course he is."

They moved into position without another word.

Lights off. Curtains open just enough to see. Breathing slowed. Hearts loud. Minutes crawled by. Then—A sound. Soft. Crunching. Footsteps in snow. Essence lifted two fingers. *Movement.*

Leila slid into the kitchen shadows, blade ready. Bailey crouched behind the couch, gun steady. Shiffon stepped into the hallway, body angled to shield her son.

Another crunch. Closer. The back fence creaked. Shiffon's pulse thundered. A shadow passed the frosted kitchen window. Then the power cut. Darkness swallowed the house.

Bailey hissed, "Now."

The back door burst inward with a sharp crack. Cold air flooded the kitchen as a figure lunged inside—

gun raised, breath fogging. Leila moved first. Her blade flashed once, slicing the man's wrist clean. His gun clattered to the floor, followed by a scream that barely escaped his throat before Essence slammed a fist into his jaw and dragged him down.

A second man crashed through the doorway. Bailey fired, low, precise, catching him in the leg. He went down hard, cursing. Shiffon didn't move. She listened. Because Riot never sent just two. A third shadow slipped through the side window, glass crunching under boots. Shiffon turned and met Riot Mercer's eyes in the dark. He stepped inside slowly, unhurried, gun loose in his hand like he wasn't even sure he'd need it.

"Merry Christmas," he said softly.

Shiffon's grip tightened around her son. "Merry fuckin' Christmas to you too."

Riot smiled. "I knew you'd stay. Mothers always do."

Essence moved into the hallway, weapon trained. "Take another step and I put you down."

Riot didn't look at her. His eyes never left Shiffon—or the baby carrier strapped to her chest.

"You finally stopped running," he said. "That's growth."

"You came for my child," Shiffon said, voice shaking with fury. "That's a death wish."

Riot tilted his head, studying the baby like he was assessing an object. "That boy is Maverick's blood. Which makes him important."

"He's not yours," Shiffon snapped.

"Everything Maverick left behind is," Riot replied calmly. "Including you."

The room tensed.

Bailey's finger tightened on the trigger.

Shiffon took one step forward. "You touch him and I won't just kill you."

Riot's lips twitched. "Very dramatic. I like that."

Outside, police sirens wailed faintly, drawn by earlier chaos, still far enough away to not matter.

Riot raised his gun, not at Shiffon but at Essence.

Leila moved instantly, hurling her blade. It struck Riot's shoulder, spinning him back with a grunt. He fired wildly, bullet punching into the ceiling. Shiffon reacted without thinking. She surged forward, slammed Riot into the wall, and drove her knee into his ribs. The baby carrier held firm—she'd tested it for this exact reason.

Riot laughed through the pain. "That's her," he wheezed. "That's the woman Maverick loved."

Essence smashed the butt of her gun into Riot's face. Blood sprayed. Riot stumbled but didn't fall. He shoved her back, grabbed his wounded shoulder, and backed toward the shattered window.

"You think this ends tonight?" he snarled. "This boy will never be safe. Not while I breathe. He belongs to me."

Shiffon raised her gun, hands steady now. "Then breathe carefully."

She fired. The bullet tore through Riot's shoulder again, spinning him backward through the broken window and into the snow outside. He hit hard, rolling once before scrambling to his feet. Sirens grew louder. Riot staggered into the storm, blood staining the white ground behind him. He looked back once, eyes wild, smiling.

"This ain't over," he called. "Not even close."

Then he disappeared into the darkness. The house fell silent except for the baby's soft stirring. Shiffon collapsed against the wall, legs trembling.

Essence rushed to her. "You, okay? He, okay?"

Shiffon nodded, breath ragged. "We're alive."

Bailey exhaled shakily. "That's... something."

Leila stared at the broken window, snow blowing in. "He's wounded."

"But not finished," Shiffon said quietly.

She looked down at her son as he opened his eyes, blinking up at her like nothing in the world was wrong.

"Merry Christmas," she whispered to him.

Outside, snow fell harder, covering blood, footprints, and promises. And somewhere in the city, Riot Mercer was still breathing.

Chapter Twelve

LET THE WINTER BURY HIM

Christmas morning arrived quietly. No sirens. No shouting. No gunfire echoing off brick and glass. Just snow. Atlanta lay buried beneath it, soft, clean, deceptive, like the city was trying to pretend nothing violent had happened the night before. The safe house smelled faintly of gun oil and coffee. Broken glass had been swept into a corner. The traps were dismantled. The adrenaline had finally drained, leaving exhaustion in its place.

Shiffon sat on the edge of the bed with her son cradled against her chest, rocking him gently. The world felt smaller this morning. Narrowed down to the steady rhythm of his breathing, the warmth of his skin, the miracle that he was still here. Alive.

Essence leaned against the doorway, arms crossed, eyes softer than usual. "He sleep?"

"Out cold," Shiffon murmured. "Guess he didn't feel the holiday chaos."

Bailey hovered nearby with a mug of coffee she hadn't touched. "News said a man was shot near here last night. No suspect. No name."

Leila sneered from the chair by the window. "Of course not. Riot ain't sloppy enough to get caught."

Shiffon didn't look up. "He wanted us to know he survived."

Essence nodded. "And he wanted you to know he ain't done."

Silence settled again. Outside, a neighbor laughed. Somewhere down the block, a radio played a gospel version of *Silent Night*. Snow slid off rooftops in soft avalanches. Life moved on, like it always did.

Shiffon kissed her son's forehead, lingering there. "I'm taking him to see my mother."

All three women turned to her at once. Today?" Bailey asked.

"Yes," Shiffon said. "Brief. Controlled. No surprises." She met their eyes, one by one. "She deserves Christmas with her grandson."

Leila tilted her head. "And Riot?"

"Riot already knows who I am," Shiffon replied.

"Hiding harder won't change that. But I won't give him access either."

Essence pushed off the doorway. "Then we do it smart."

○○○

Shiffon stood on the porch she grew up on, snow crunching under her boots. Her mother opened the door before Shiffon could knock, like she'd been waiting all morning.

"Oh my God," her mother whispered again, just like the night before.

Shiffon smiled this time. "Morning, Ma."

Her brother appeared behind her mother, eyes lighting up instantly. "That's my nephew."

Shiffon stepped inside, warmth wrapping around them. She gently pulled back the blanket.

Her mother gasped, pressing both hands to her chest. "Lord have mercy..."

She touched the baby's cheek with reverence, tears spilling freely now. "He looks like you. Strong."

Shiffon exhaled, something loosening in her chest that had been tight for months.

They sat together on the couch, no weapons visible, no paranoia allowed for just a moment. Her mother hummed softly, rocking the baby like she'd done a thousand times before. Her brother snapped pictures, swearing he wouldn't post them anywhere.

"I knew you weren't gone," her mother whispered. "A mother knows."

Shiffon closed her eyes. "I'm here now."

But not for long. When she left, hugging them tighter than she meant to, her mother held her face in both hands.

"Whatever you got tangled up in," she said firmly, "don't let it touch him."

Shiffon nodded. "I won't."

She meant it.

○○○

Riot Mercer sat in the back of a stolen sedan, shoulder bandaged, teeth clenched against the ache. Blood still stained the inside of his coat. His reflection in the window looked wilder now, edges sharpened by pain and humiliation. He smiled anyway.

"She didn't kill me," he muttered.

The driver glanced back nervously. "Boss... you sure this worth it?"

Riot's eyes gleamed. "Maverick left a son." He leaned forward, voice low and sure. "And that boy gon' grow up knowing who controls his legacy. Only way to do that is for me to raise him as my own son. Maverick would want it that way," Riot convinced himself.

Snow blurred the windshield as the car disappeared into traffic. Winter hadn't buried him. It had baptized him.

○○○

Back at the safe house, Shiffon stood by the window again, watching snow fall under streetlights. Her son slept peacefully in his bassinet, unaware that his name already carried weight in a world built on blood.

Essence joined her. "You good?"

Shiffon nodded slowly. "I'm done running."

Bailey raised her mug. "To surviving Christmas."

Leila smirked. "And ruining everybody else's."

Shiffon smiled—small, fierce, unafraid.

Outside, the snow kept falling, covering footprints, hiding scars, muting echoes of violence. But winter didn't erase memory. And this one? This one would remember them.

EPILOGUE...

SOME GHOSTS STILL WATCH

Night fell early, the way it always did in winter. Shiffon sat alone in the living room of the safe house, lights low, her son asleep against her chest. Essence and the others had stepped out to grab food—something warm, something normal, for the first time in days. Snow drifted lazily past the window. For a few rare, fragile minutes... everything was still. Her phone vibrated softly in her hand. She frowned. **No caller ID.** Her thumb hovered. Every instinct she had told her not to answer. She did anyway.

"Hello?"

Silence.

Then a familiar voice—low, measured, careful. "Tell me the rumors aren't true."

Shiffon's breath caught.

"...Caleb?"

He exhaled sharply on the other end, relief and frustration tangled together. "Tell me you didn't come back. Tell me you didn't walk back into the fire with that baby when you know damn well it's not safe."

Shiffon leaned back against the couch, eyes closing. "It's Christmas."

"That's not an answer."

"I'm alive," she said softly. "He's alive. And for today? That's enough."

Caleb's voice dropped. "You don't understand what you've started all over again."

"I understand exactly what I've started," Shiffon replied. "But I'm done living like I'm already dead."

A pause. Longer this time.

"I bought you time," Caleb said. "I risked everything to make sure nobody ever came looking for you and your son."

"I know," Shiffon whispered. "And I'll never forget that."

Another breath on the line. Heavy. Protective. "Just... be careful," he said. "For his sake."

"I always am," she answered. The call ended.

Shiffon stared at the dark screen for a long moment, then set the phone face-down on the table. Outside, the snow kept falling. She looked down at her son, his tiny fist curled against her sweater, his face peaceful and unaware of how many men had already decided his future.

"Tomorrow," she murmured, pressing a kiss to his hair. "I'll worry about tomorrow, tomorrow."

For tonight, she let herself believe in the miracle.

Because Christmas didn't promise safety. It promised survival. And in this world. That was everything.

A KING PRODUCTION

Toxic...

A Titillating Tale

A Novelette

JOY DEJA KING

Chapter One

LOVE HATE

Got Time Today

"Look at that trifling nigga right there," Harper seethed. "He about to make me fuck my nails up." She glanced down at her freshly done, blush pink mountain peak nails with rhinestone swirls, as her fury continuied to simmer.

"Girl, let's just go. You don't need this drama. You got plenty of other options. You won't have no problem replacing him. Fuck Jamari!" Taliyah was doing her best to get her friend to leave the scene, but it wasn't working. When Harper got amped up, there was nothing nobody could do to lower her temperature.

"Nah, fuck that." Harper's tone had turned calm

but icy, which only meant she was about to raise hell. "He ain't about to play me out here in these streets." She grabbed her purse and quickly jumped out her car with Taliyah trailing behind her.

Amina make me so sick! Why the hell did she have to call Harper and let her know Jamari was up in Phipps Plaza shopping wit' the next chick, Taliyah thought to herself as she watched Harper approach her boyfriend.

"What's good?!" Harper popped, sounding more like a dude than the prissy princess her outer appearance exuded. It was the main reason she always had problems with men. They thought they would be dating some submissive eye candy. By the time they realized she had the mindset of a nigga, who just so happened to look good in a dress, it was too late.

"Baby, what you doing here?" Jamari asked nervously, as he was putting shopping bags in the trunk of his car.

"I see you did some shopping. What you buy me?" Harper questioned, grabbing one of the Louis Vuitton bags.

"Umm, that's mine!" The chick with Jamari shouted trying to snatch the bag out Harper's hand.

"I advise you to let go of this bag, and stay the fuck outta this. This between me and Jamari. You don't want this smoke....I promise you," Harper warned.

The girl didn't know anything about Harper, but her instincts told her the bitch was crazy. So she stepped back, and directed her attention back to the man who had just taken her on a shopping spree. Her first one at that. She didn't want to mess things up with him, but she wasn't trying to scrap in the mall parking lot either.

"Jamari, what's going on... and who is she?" the girl smacked, folding her arms with an attitude.

"Yeah Jamari, who am I?" Harper smirked, enjoying how rattled he was. Although he was trying to act like he had everything under control, his eyes were telling a different story.

"Baby, let me speak to you for a minute." Jamari spoke smoothly, reaching out his hand, and gently taking Harper's arm.

"Get tha fuck off me!" She barked, yanking her arms out his grasp, before pulling out her baby Glock, that she never left home without.

"Yo, yo, yo!" Jamari put his hands up, slowly stepping back.

"I knew that bitch was crazy," the girl who was with Jamari mumbled, shaking her head. Her first thought was to get her phone and call the police, but quickly realized she had already put her purse in the car. She didn't want to draw unwanted attention to herself by opening the passenger door, so she remained in the background quiet.

"Harper, put the gun away and let's go," Taliyah sighed. She was used to her friend's antics but the shit was draining.

"You can go wait in the car for me, 'cause I got

time today. We ain't done here, but this won't take much longer," Harper told her friend, keeping her gun aimed at Jamari.

"Baby, please calm down," Jamari pleaded, keeping his hands up. "It's not what you think. You know I love you."

"You so full of shit," Harper laughed wickedly. "It's always you pretty boys that think you can sweet talk yo' way out some lies."

Harper continued to laugh as she began grabbing the pricey items out of the shopping bags. One-by-one, she tossed them in the mud puddles that hadn't dried up from the storm the night before.

"No you fuckin' didn't!" The girl with Jamari screamed. Horrified seeing the luxury goods she envisioned showing off on the Gram being ruined, right in front of her eyes.

"Yo Harper, I can't believe you doing this dumb shit!" He roared, finally losing his cool. Jamari started to storm toward her, until she raised that Glock, aiming it firmly at his chest.

"Back tha fuck up, or else," Harper threatened, nodding her head, tossing out the last bag from the trunk. But she wasn't done yet. She reached back in her purse and brandished the knife she always kept on her too. She proceeded to walk around Jamari's brand new black on black Camaro Coupe ZL1 and slashed each tire.

"You bitch! I'ma fuck you up!" Jamari uttered viciously, ready to break Harper's neck. But she wasn't worried. She was the one holding the gun.

"Ya lovebirds can walk the fuck home, hand in hand. So who's the bitch now," Harper mocked, going back to her car.

"Harper, you are fuckin' certifiable, like seriously," Taliyah kept repeating as she stared back looking at Jamari. He was having a complete meltdown, while the girl he was with, was picking up purses, shoes and clothes, trying to salvage whatever items she could.

"Jamari betta be happy I didn't bust out them windows and key his car too," she snarled. "I bet that nigga learned today not to disrespect me," Harper scoffed, driving off.

A. KING PRODUCTION

Yacht Girl

*Behind every
yacht, is a secret...*

A Novelette

JOY DEJA KING

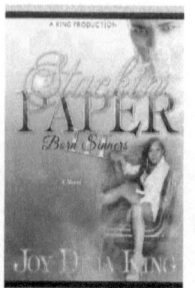

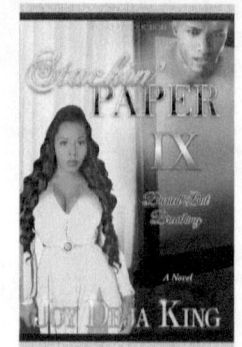

A KING PRODUCTION

Stackin'
PAPER

a novel

JOY DEJA KING

Chapter One
A Killer Is Born

Philly, 1993

"Please, Daquan, don't hit me again!" the young mother screamed, covering her face in defense mode. She hurriedly pushed herself away from her predator, sliding her body on the cold hardwood floor.

"Bitch, get yo' ass back over here!" he barked, grabbing her matted black hair and dragging her into the kitchen. He reached for the hot skillet from the top of the oven, and you could hear the oil popping underneath the fried chicken his wife had been cooking right before he came home. "Didn't I tell you to have my food ready on the table when I came home?"

"I… I… I was almost finished, but you came home early," Teresa stuttered, "Ouch!" she yelled as her neck damn near snapped when Daquan gripped her hair even tighter.

"I don't want to hear your fuckin' excuses. That's what yo' problem is. You so damn hard headed and neva want to listen. But like they say, a hard head make fo' a soft ass. You gon' learn to listen to me."

"Please, please, Daquan, don't do this! Let me finish frying your chicken and I'll never do this again. Your food will be ready and on the table everyday on time. I promise!"

"I'm tired of hearing your damn excuses."

"Bang!" was all you heard as the hot skillet came crashing down on Teresa's head. The hot oil splashed up in the air, and if Daquan hadn't moved forward and turned his head, his face would've been saturated with the grease.

But Teresa wasn't so lucky, as the burning oil grazed her hands, as they were protecting her face and part of her thigh.

After belting out in pain from the grease, she then noticed blood trickling down from the open gash on the side of her forehead. But it didn't stop there. Daquan then put the skillet down and began kicking Teresa in her ribs and back like she was a diseased infected dog that had just bitten him.

"Yo', Pops, leave moms alone! Why you always got to do this? It ain't never no peace when you come in this house." Genesis stood in the kitchen entrance with his fists clenched and panting like a bull. He had grown sick and tired of watching his father beat his mother down almost every single day. At the age of eleven he had seen his mother receive more ass whippings than hugs or any indication of love.

"Boy, who the fuck you talkin' to? You betta get yo' ass back in your room and stay the hell outta of grown people's business."

"Genesis, listen to your father. I'll be alright. Now go

back to your room," his mother pleaded.

Genesis just stood there unable to move, watching his mother and feeling helpless. The blood was now covering her white nightgown and she was covering her midsection, obviously in pain trying to protect the baby that was growing inside of her. He was in a trance, not knowing what to do to make the madness stop. But he was quickly brought back to reality when he felt his jaw almost crack from the punch his father landed on the side of his face.

"I ain't gon' tell you again. Get yo' ass back in your room! And don't come out until I tell you to! Now go!" Daquan didn't even wait to let his only son go back to his room. He immediately went over to Teresa and picked up where he left off, punishing her body with punches and kicks. He seemed oblivious to the fact that not only was he killing her, but also he was killing his unborn child right before his son's eyes.

A tear streamed down Genesis's face as he tried to reflect on one happy time he had with his dad, but he went blank. There were no happy times. From the first moment he could remember, his dad was a monster.

All Genesis remembered starting from the age of three was the constant beat downs his mother endured for no reason. If his dad's clothes weren't ironed just right, then a blow to the face. If the volume of the television was too loud, then a jab here. And, God forbid, if the small, two-bedroom apartment in the drug-infested building they lived in wasn't spotless, a nuclear bomb would explode in the form of Daquan. But the crazy part was, no matter how clean their apartment was or how good the food was cooked and his clothes being ironed just right, it was never good enough. Daquan would bust in the door, drunk or high, full of anger, ready to take out all his frustration out on his wife. The dead end jobs, being broke, living in the drug infested and violent prone city of Philadelphia had turned the already troubled man into poison to his whole family.

"Daddy, leave my mom alone," Genesis said in a calm, unemotional tone. Daquan kept striking Teresa as if he didn't hear his son. "I'm not gonna to tell you again. Leave my mom alone." This time Daquan heard his son's warning but seemed unfazed.

"I guess that swollen jaw wasn't enough for you. You dying to get that ass beat." Daquan looked down at a now black and blue Teresa who seemed to be about to take her last breath. "You keep yo' ass right here, while I teach our son a lesson." Teresa reached her hand out with the little strength she had left trying to save her son. But she quickly realized it was too late. The sins of the parents had now falling upon their child.

"Get away from my mother. I want you to leave and don't ever come back."

Daquan was so caught up in the lashing he had been putting on his wife that he didn't even notice Genesis retrieving the gun he left on the kitchen counter until he had it raised and pointed in his direction. "Lil' fuck, you un lost yo' damn mind! You gon' make me beat you with the tip of my gun."

Daquan reached his hand out to grab the gun out of Genesis's hand, and when he moved his leg forward, it would be the last step he'd ever take in his life. The single shot fired ripped through Daquan's heart and he collapsed on the kitchen floor, dying instantly.

Genesis was frozen and his mother began crying hysterically.

"Oh dear God!" Teresa moaned, trying to gasp for air. "Oh, Genesis baby, what have you done?" She stared at Daquan, who laid face up with his eyes wide open in shock. He died not believing until it was too late that his own son would be the one to take him out this world.

It wasn't until they heard the pounding on the front door that Genesis snapped back to the severity of the situation at hand.

"Is everything alright in there?" they heard the older lady from across the hall ask.

Genesis walked to the door still gripping the .380-caliber semi-automatic. He opened the door and said in a serene voice, "No, Ms. Johnson, everything is *not* alright. I just killed my father."

****

Two months later, Teresa cried as she watched her son being taking away to spend a minimum of two years in a juvenile facility in Pemberton, New Jersey.

Although it was obvious by the bruises on both Teresa and Genesis that he acted in self defense, the judge felt that the young boy having to live with the guilt of murdering his own father wasn't punishment enough. He concluded that if Genesis didn't get a hard wake up call, he would be headed on a path of self destruction. He first ordered him to stay at the juvenile facility until he was eighteen. But after pleas from his mother, neighbors and his teacher, who testified that Genesis had the ability to accomplish whatever he wanted in life because of how smart and gifted he was, the judge reduced it to two years, but only if he demonstrated excellent behavior during his time there. Those two years turned into four and four turned into seven. At the age of eighteen when Genesis was finally released he was no longer a young boy, he was now a criminal minded man.

P.O. Box 912
Collierville, TN 38027
🌸🌸🌸🌸🌸🌸🌸🌸🌸🌸🌸🌸🌸

A KING PRODUCTION

www.joydejaking.com
@preciouscummingsofficial
🌸🌸🌸🌸🌸🌸🌸🌸🌸🌸🌸🌸🌸

ORDER FORM

Name:

Address:

City/State:

Zip:

QUANTITY	TITLES	PRICE	TOTAL
	Bitch	$17.99	
	Bitch Reloaded	$17.99	
	The Bitch Is Back	$17.99	
	Queen Bitch	$17.99	
	Last Bitch Standing	$17.99	
	Superstar	$17.99	
	Ride Wit' Me	$17.99	
	Ride Wit' Me Part 2	$17.99	
	Stackin' Paper	$17.99	
	Trife Life To Lavish	$17.99	
	Trife Life To Lavish II	$17.99	
	Stackin' Paper II	$17.99	
	Rich or Famous	$17.99	
	Rich or Famous Part 2	$17.99	
	Rich or Famous Part 3	$17.99	
	Bitch A New Beginning	$17.99	
	Mafia Princess Part 1	$17.99	
	Mafia Princess Part 2	$17.99	
	Mafia Princess Part 3	$17.99	
	Mafia Princess Part 4	$17.99	
	Mafia Princess Part 5	$17.99	
	Boss Bitch	$17.99	
	Baller Bitches Vol. 1	$17.99	
	Baller Bitches Vol. 2	$17.99	
	Baller Bitches Vol. 3	$17.99	
	Bad Bitch	$17.99	
	Still The Baddest Bitch	$17.99	
	Power	$17.99	
	Power Part 2	$17.99	
	Drake	$17.99	
	Drake Part 2	$17.99	
	Female Hustler	$17.99	
	Female Hustler Part 2	$17.99	
	Female Hustler Part 3	$17.99	

QUANTITY	TITLES	PRICE	TOTAL
	Female Hustler Part 4	$17.99	
	Female Hustler Part 5	$17.99	
	Female Hustler Part 6	$17.99	
	Princess Fever "Birthday Bash"	$6.00	
	Nico Carter The Men Of The Bitch Series	$17.99	
	Bitch The Beginning Of The End	$17.99	
	Supreme...Men Of The Bitch Series	$17.99	
	Bitch The Final Chapter	$17.99	
	Stackin' Paper III	$17.99	
	Men Of The Bitch Series And The Women Who Love Them	$17.99	
	Coke Like The 80s	$17.99	
	Baller Bitches The Reunion Vol. 4	$17.99	
	Stackin' Paper IV	$17.99	
	The Legacy	$17.99	
	Lovin' Thy Enemy	$17.99	
	Stackin' Paper V	$17.99	
	The Legacy Part 2	$17.99	
	Assassins - Episode 1	$12.99	
	Assassins - Episode 2	$12.99	
	Assassins - Episode 3	$12.99	
	Bitch Chronicles	$40.00	
	So Hood So Rich	$17.99	
	Stackin' Paper VI	$17.99	
	Female Hustler Part 7	$17.99	
	Toxic...	$12.99	
	Stackin' Paper VII	$17.99	
	Sugar Babies...	$12.99	
	Deadly Divorce...	$12.99	
	The Legacy Part 3	$17.99	
	BITCH The Story of Precious Cummings	$17.99	
	Mastermind...	$12.99	
	Stackin' Paper VIII	$17.99	
	Stackin' Paper Holiday	$12.99	
	Mastermind 2...	$12.99	
	Baller Bitches Vol. 5	$17.99	
	Mastermind 3...	$12.99	
	Trife Life To Lavish III	$17.99	
	Stackin' Paper IX	$17.99	
	Assassins Holiday- Episode 4	$11.00	

Shipping/Handling (Via Priority Mail) $11.00 1-3 Books, $19.99 4-10 Books. For 11 or more $24.75.
Total: $_____FORMS OF ACCEPTED PAYMENTS: Certified or government issued checks and
money Orders, all mail in orders take 5-7 Business days to be delivered

www.ingramcontent.com/pod-product-compliance
Lightning Source LLC
Chambersburg PA
CBHW030536180626
46810CB00005B/1900